Charles Chauncy Haven

Thirty Days in New Jersey Ninety Years Ago

Charles Chauncy Haven

Thirty Days in New Jersey Ninety Years Ago

ISBN/EAN: 9783337401733

Printed in Europe, USA, Canada, Australia, Japan

Cover: Foto ©Andreas Hilbeck / pixelio.de

More available books at **www.hansebooks.com**

OLD DAYS IN NEW JERSEY

NINETY YEARS AGO:

AN ESSAY

GIVING NEW FACTS IN CONNECTION WITH

THIRTY DAYS IN NEW JERSEY NINETY YEARS AGO.

THOSE who believe that all the wonderful events in the world have occurred in their time, need not be invited to have their delusions dissipated by a perusal of this humble Essay. Nor need those fastidious Novel-fanciers, who detest a story founded on fact, expect to have their love of pure fiction gratified by what I shall venture to prove. Ninety years ago in this country, when, Hercules-like, our young Republic leaped from its cradle to wrestle for its life with the British lion, was not a time for idle sport or ordinary enterprises. Later experiences on a larger scale, and our recent gigantic Rebel war especially, which the athletic maturity of the loyal sons of our great country has been able to terminate successfully, cannot, ought not to be underrated. But, if there ever was a period that really tried men's souls and bodies with intense suffering and fortitude, the wonderful events in New Jersey in the campaigns of 1776 and 1777 may fairly challenge contemplation. History is full of these gloomy revelations—but all has not yet been told—nay more, a part of them could not have been prudentially revealed by Washington in that agonizing crisis, when the success of our Independence rested solely upon the pivot carried in his bosom, and almost instant perdition seemed to overwhelm the glorious cause, whose triumph has since revolutionized so great a part of the world.

It is not to glorify this epoch above all other events in our country's earlier or later achievements that I undertake to gather together a few of the lost Sibyl leaves of the Revolutionary history. I seek only to do justice to what occurred in this part of New Jersey in the gloomy period which was the turning point where the fortunes of our young Republic were reversed, and when some suppressed details caused what has been called a "*casus omissus*" in the official reports published at the time. Facts have been since revealed and fully corroborated in regard to the second engagement in Trenton, which took place on the banks of the Assunpink, which demonstrate it to have been a much more important fight in its consequences, as well as strategic skill and bravery, than that of the surprise of the Hessians, or the gallant but much more costly victory at Princeton.

Credence of this fact, however, at this time is hard to be secured. It is a matter of surprise that many readers have never heard so much as that there was any battle on the 2d of January 1777, and that others only conceived it to be a cannonade. But Lord Cornwallis[*] did not even admit in his official report that he ever approached the bridge where the struggle was, and Washington[†] scarcely alluded to his position there (being one that would not bear to be disclosed at the time), although he afterwards alluded to it as one of the most perilous and memorable events of the war. 'See Trumbulls Memoirs and Picture of the battle at the Bridge, and

* See Appendix.   † See Appendix.

Washington's letter to the matrons and maidens who welcomed him there in 1789.' Even our early Historians said but little about it, making the capture of the Hessians on the 26th of December 1776, and the victory at Princeton on the 3d of January 1777, the glorious Phenix-like events of the Revolution, reviving hope and reversing despair.

In later years, it is true, some of our distinguished readers and writers of history have had the veil lifted before their eyes, and have cautiously admitted there must have been at least a bloody skirmish, or a severe repulse on that bridge, and at that ford below it, which Lord Cornwallis' generals told him he ought to take at night-fall, and not to leave until next morning. But no one has yet done justice to the real combat, by which he was so roughly handled and out-generalled, excepting the cotemporary witnesses who were in or saw the battle. Their evidence will be herein produced.

A retrospect of ninety years, and a faithful collation of facts, put together like Mosaic work, and agreeing so as to make a marvellous and yet true and consistent whole, ought to command attention. But as a mistake is considered by some writers as worse than an ordinary fault, some will not be convinced against their will. But I design, nevertheless, showing even *them* my proofs, and if they are not convinced let them be unconvinced still.

Post-mortem examinations often reveal truths that are hid from living *savans*. But the operator must beware that his own hands are without a scratch. Dead blood is dangerous to handle. I shall proceed cautiously in probing for truth, and if it is found all I ask is an acknowledgment from those who are bold enough to admit it, in spite of prejudice or partiality.

It is the prerogative of the Historian to tell the truth and the whole truth; to develop the events of the past for the benefit of future times, in a clear, impartial and accurate manner.

He should be comprehensive without redundancy— impressive without devious ostentation, but emphatically instructive without impairing the interest of the narrative, so that it can be remembered and appreciated by the reader when left to his judgment to decide upon it according to the evidence produced.

In this enlightened age readers of history will examine facts and principles and judge for themselves, and should be furnished with references and proofs that have guided the historian. He might be deemed supercilious who, fallible himself, would deny this to others. Consistent circumstances do not lie, but what narrator is always true to himself when prejudice or misapprehension may bias his pen? Even Voltaire showed this obliquity. His first life of Charles the XIIth made that hero the great man worthy to be glorified in history ; but in his second edition, influenced, it is said, by the Empress Catharine the First, he calls Peter the Great, " beaucoup plus grand homme que lui."

Even Time, which is called the test of Truth may long conceal errors, hoary with antiquity, a fact which was made manifest by the revelations of Columbus, Copernicus, Galileo, Newton and others. Let stolid criticism put on her screws and insist that

" What has been, spite of Jove himself, has been,"

but the world moves. If what I have to prove in this

Essay regarding what took place in Trenton during the *thirty days ninety years ago,* cannot be proved let it not be believed. Judicial and legislative judgments sometimes are reversed, but in regard to the authorities now believed to be in error, there will be no occasion to impugn their motives or their known integrity. Certainly not by me.

These premises being stated and admitted as necessary to enable me to proceed with frankness and fidelity in my Essay, I beg leave to state briefly its

ORIGIN AND DESIGN.

Twenty years ago, a native of Portsmouth, New Hampshire, (where was the first outbreak of the Revolutionary war in 1774,) I became a resident in New Jersey and settled at Trenton, with a New England curiosity prone to investigate and enjoy its classical associations connected with early American history, I found much of an interesting nature not authentically published, and some facts unrevealed, or misstated.

In 1855 I had collected and arranged in a consistent and credible form an analysis of events connected with remarks historical and explanatory, based on cotemporary evidences referred to, which in 1856 were read before the Literary and Philosophical Society of this city, and published. The Address was entitled, " WASHINGTON AND HIS ARMY." It was novel, and thought somewhat mythical in some of its revelations, but it was fearlessly sent to several of our historical writers and societies, and I had the satisfaction then of receiving the thanks of such societies and of such distinguished men as Irving

Bancroft, Lossing. Professor Silliman, senior, and President Felton, of Harvard College, as well as others whom I should be proud to name. With this approval of so humble an essay, and the pamphlet being all disposed of, and now out of print, I ought to have been satisfied. But this not being the case, as some of the prominent facts are not authentically admitted by some historians, although most of them are, and as I have since discovered many new proofs of their correctness, I feel at liberty to make a new Digest of what is relevant to the matters in question, quoting freely from my own publications, as abovenamed, as well as my "ANNALS OF TRENTON," published here this year, and also placing before my readers all my proofs and references, leaving the whole subject to their decision, and the candor of a liberal criticism. What I published in my 70th year, and what I have since found confirmed and can find no cause to doubt in my 80th, must be my apology for persevering in an undertaking called for by some of my friends, who think that the correctness of my statements and revelations, so interesting to Jerseymen, and particularly to Trentonians, should be fully acknowledged.

I will now proceed with the narratives.

WASHINGTON'S RETREAT INTO PENNSYLVANIA AND RETURN TO NEW JERSEY TO SURPRISE THE HESSIANS.

It was on the 8th day of December 1776, when the Army was got safely across the Delaware, and the boats were all sent up the river and secured on its western banks. It was a Pass-over long to be remembered.

Washington, whose retreat into Pennsylvania, being almost without an army, created a foreboding terror over the whole land, managed still to secure himself from his pursuers. Howe and his generals were baffled. and giving up the final victory for the present, they posted the hireling Hessians to watch our troops and plunder the inhabitants. But our lion-hearted chief was not long quiet in his lair. Turning back upon his pursuers, he soon captured most of the Hessians and drove the British into narrow quarters. Rest. however. was needed for his fatigued and almost abandoned army. Their sufferings were partially relieved; but for him there was no rest, no relief. He had to uphold and carry Independence almost solely upon his own shoulders. For Washington there could be no substitute.

Let those who would have a more comprehensive view of the sufferings he and his army endured at this time, read Bancroft's ninth volume. particularly chapters 12th, 13th and 14th. They treat of the wonderful days in New Jersey.

I quote now from my own Address : pp. 20–28.

" In that portentous exigency, when every ray of hope appeared to have abandoned the wavering and frightened masses of the people. and a gloom like that of a sudden and unexpected night had settled on all below and around him, his eagle eye was soaring still higher and higher, to keep its steady gaze upon the departing day; and thus from his habitual trust in God and the light of conscious rectitude in his cause, it seemed as if

' Eternal sunshine settled on his head.' "

He had to deal. however, with so many mortal calami-

2

ties, that neither the pen of a Bancroft, nor Irving's feeling narration, nor Leutze's nor Sully's pencil could portray his embarrassments.

"Besides these disheartening circumstances, the Commander-in-chief had his own private griefs to contend with—dissatisfaction, disobedience and desertion of some of those highest in favor in the army and who became so in the country generally, because they had been successful, and he was not—they had reaped laurels which others had won for them—and he had lost them because his chance of obtaining them was frustrated by insuperable difficulties, and because like Fabius, he preferred securing victory by fortitude, prudence and delay, rather than rashly risking everything to exhibit what they called decision! General Lee (since proved a Traitor) refused moving to his assistance, after reiterated orders and remonstrances; but, as if to clip his self-importance, he was soon afterwards taken a prisoner by his own folly and imprudence. Gates preferred deserting him at his utmost need and going to Congress to suggest his own plan for saving the country—and, worse than all, his own 'bosom's oracle,' his Marcus Brutus, in the camp and in council, the friend who absolutely had the love of such a heart as Washington's (I name him not), at that moment faltered in his confidence in him, and if he had not promptly repented of his folly and injustice, he would thereby have fixed an eternal stigma on his own hitherto unsullied character. Washington was only exalted the more by all these pitiable misgivings. What he knew of them he overlooked and forgave; but he did not know all."

My intimations ten years ago have turned out correct.

It is proved by "Donop's Diary," according to Mr. Bancroft. vol. , page 22 , and other evidence, that Colonel Reed went over to the enemy's camp and took a pardon, about the time Washington was crossing the Delaware. He afterwards tried to conceal this, and recover his lost honor. But such a leap in the darkest hour, and back again the next day when light broke upon our benighted cause, although it might serve to satisfy his own idea of being all right, did not (and in spite of his lineal panegyrist), cannot satisfy others. Still let him be remembered gratefully for his services, and let his proud, treacherous, and unenviable character pass out of memory as soon as possible.

The Commander-in-chief consumed a few days in maturing his plans for future operations. Among other things not yet told in our histories, he ordered up a company of hardy long-shore riggers, sail and block makers, consisting of eighty-two young men, all less than twenty-three years old, under the brave Captain Moulder, of Philadelphia, whose battery of two guns, long four-inch pieces, did so much gallant service at the battles of the Assunpink and Princeton. This fact was communicated to me by the son of Lieutenant Cuthburt, of Philadelphia, whose father was afterwards Captain of the same company; whose commission was exhibited to me signed by Colonel Joseph Reed.

Cornwallis, after posting about twenty-five hundred Hessians, under Colonels Rahl and Dunop, all along the Trenton side of the Delaware, to watch Washington's movements, or pardon the frightened inhabitants, prepared to go to England to assure his Royal master that the Revolution was quelled, and Peace with his loving Colonists was likely to be soon settled on a surer basis than ever.

"Congress at the same time appeared to be alarmed for their safety, and resolved to adjourn to Baltimore. Even the cradle of Independence in Philadelphia seemed almost within the grasp of the enemy, and the example and the watchfulness of the brave old Putnam could hardly preserve order in that city of brotherly love, nor restore the lost confidence in the success of our arms anywhere. Everything seemed to go wrong." * * *

"Fortunately for the country, Washington possessed a spirit that seemed not only invulnerable to disaster, but so tenacious of success eventually, that victory and independence were always cherished guests in his bosom, never to be abandoned. Congress, therefore, transferred their waning confidence in the cause to his care, and invested him with almost dictatorial powers. How safe this trust was in his keeping, history has told!

"He began immediately to make use of it. His retreat thus far, which military men give him now great credit for, was looked upon, *at the time*, as most disastrous; but even before it was accomplished, his thoughtful mind was then meditating a reaction upon the foe.
  *   *   *   *   *   *

"His first scheme was now to be tried—to fall upon the harpies that were pursuing him, and to clip their wings whilst distended. The time was come to attempt something on their unguarded outposts, to show that he was not wanting in decision, and to convince the country that it was necessary to turn upon their invaders, to punish and drive out the brutal Hessians, whose lustful and rapacious soldiery spared neither age nor sex, whigs nor tories. A vigorous resistance, he thought, would rouse the drooping spirits of the people in this and other States, and induce some of them to abandon the royal standard, and return to help their own countrymen whom they had so cravenly deserted."

The remnants of the old army, reduced to less than three thousand men, mustered on the west side of the Delaware, were in the most destitute and suffering condition.

"It was so heart-rending, it would not be tolerated for a moment in our days, and scarcely can be believed by us. In our comfortable homes, well clothed, and warmed, and fed, many of us, by our own parlor firesides, surrounded with almost every luxury that wealth and taste can supply—how can we realize what we have never felt, and actually know nothing about? I speak of those who often experienced absolute hunger, sparingly allayed by tainted meat and mouldy bread— marching and fasting for nights and days together, weary, suffering, fainting, perhaps with bleeding feet, or attacks of small-pox, which was then prevalent, encountering snow, rain, or hail, with ragged, shabby clothing, not being provided, generally, with shoes or stockings or tents, or cooking utensils, or money to buy anything with!

"With this motley array of an army, of about five thousand men, including raw recruits, and ill fitted for duty or discipline, Washington was emboldened to make his celebrated *coup de main* on the Hessians at Trenton. By this strategem he hoped to relieve New Jersey from their ravages, to prevent Philadelphia from falling into the hands of the British, and to rouse the

drooping spirits of the country, which were now at their
lowest ebb.

"This force was divided into three separate corps, of
which Washington had under his command about two
thousand four hundred men; General Ewing and General Cadwalader, with the remainder, were to co-operate,
by simultaneous attacks, at Trenton Ferry and at Bristol,
whilst Washington was to cross at McKonkey's Ferry,
where the boats, under the charge of Colonel Glover
(who General Wilkinson states was here), with the Mar-
blehead fishermen, had been got in readiness. These
hardy, sea-bred soldiers (together with Moulder's boys,
and Captain John Blunt, whom, according to the "Ram-
bles of Portsmuth," page 263, Washington asked to take
the helm,) were engaged for ten eventful hours in ferry-
ing over the last reserved hopes and fortunes of our country, through the booming ice-crags of that stormy Christmas night. Without the aid of these brave fishermen and
the stentorian lungs of General Knox, it is admitted the
army, with its artillery, could not have been got over,
nor could the splendid results which followed, which
turned the night of despair into a day of rejoicing
throughout the country have been realized.

"I shall not attempt to give a description of the
attack and capture of the Hessians in this city, every
particular of which is as familiar as household words to
you all. The conception, execution, and beneficial influence of this successful enterprise have an epic grandeur
in our history, worthy the pen of genius, and the pencil
of our best painters to portray. Suffice it for me to say,
Washington commanded, Greene, Sullivan, St. Clair,
Mercer, Sterling, Knox, Dickinson, Stevens, Wilkinson,

Stark. Hamilton. Baylor, McPherson. Glover. Forest, Monroe, Captains Washington, Frelinghuysen.[*] Mott, Moore. Moulder. and others of our brave officers, and about two thousand four hundred of our hardiest and most reliable troops all did their duty that night. and after taking about one thousand of the Hessians prisoners. with their colors. cannon, stores, &c., breakfasted in their camp and then returned on the same day, by the same road they came, to the other side of the Delaware."

In addition to the foregoing succinct account of the engagement at Trenton. I think it will be acceptable to my general readers to republish what has appeared in my " ANNALS OF THE CITY OF TRENTON," printed here last year. They were written in a more free and familiar style than is usual in historic narratives. but they contain graphic details and interesting anecdotes that may be thought pertinent to the correct illustration of the marvellous, or rather Providential events that occurred in this quarter in 1776, making the first Christmas night of our young Republic the most memorable of any that has ever occurred in this quarter:

" It has been a subject of some uncertainty, but of much interest to Trentonians, how and where the Hessians were captured. We will here give a condensed account of the result of our critical investigation of the historical and local statements of this most important event. When the two divisions of Washington's army entered the town, about 8 o'clock on the morning of the 26th of December, 1776, Colonel Rahl's forces were off their guard and much scattered. It was Washington's

---

* It was Captain, afterwards General, Frelinghuysen. who, it is stated, shot General Rahl with a musket, but this is doubtful.

design to entrap them, as well as all the British forces
at Mount Holly and elsewhere under Count Dunop;
but the failure of Ewing's and Cadwalader's two detach-
ments of our army to get across the Delaware, defeated
a part of this bold and complete plan. Washington, on
arriving at the entrance of the town where Warren and
Greene streets (then King and Queen) unite, came down
Warren with his artillery and the greater part of his
division, which had entered by the Pennington road, but
he sent a detachment under Colonel Hand down Greene
street to prevent the enemy from escaping to Princeton.

The first conflict with the main part of the Hessians,
who were endeavoring to form into line with a battery, took place near the head of Warren street, where
Captain William Washington (afterwards the distinguished partisan officer) and Lieutenant Monroe (the
future President of the United States) were successful,
with a few brave men, in capturing two of the enemy's
guns, which were afterwards turned upon them. Thus
repulsed, they scattered and ran across to Greene street.
General Sullivan's division, with Stark in the advance,
had rushed through Willow street and along Front
towards the bridge that crossed the Assunpink at the
foot of Greene street. Only the dragoons and a few
light horse escaped over it towards Bordentown. The
Hessians had to turn back in that quarter, and with
Colonel Rahl's other forces, whom he was trying to form
into something like a line, were forced back by Washington's division, and finally huddled together in an old
apple orchard which extended from Academy and
Hanover streets, towards where the Canal now is, and
eastward to the Assunpink. Here, between Montgom-

ery and Stockton streets, east of the old Quaker Church, Washington was about directing, in person, a discharge of cannister shot from Morgan's battery upon the disordered and bewildered Hessians, whose commander had been mortally wounded, when, according to General Wilkinson, who was a witness of the morning's encoun. ter, Captain Morgan told Washington they had *struck!* Their colors were down, and they had grounded their muskets. Raising his arms and being satisfied of the fact, he exclaimed, " Why so they have," and galloped towards them. The bleeding and vanquished Colonel Rahl, no longer the dreaded master of this important post, but unhorsed and dying, gave up his sword to General Washington, at that moment pre-eminently the savior of his country.

"Americans! imagine his emotions at that exciting and auspicious event. Success had seemed to have abandoned the proud cause for which he had risked his life, his fortune, and his fame ; and instead of disastrous battles and almost hopeless retreats ever since he had left New England, here was his first signal triumph to reward him for his brave perseverance, and his comrades for their long-endured sufferings, fidelity and patriotism. Imagine the heartfelt burst of exultation Washington and the brave band with him felt at that ecstatic moment. From " Freedom's dying embers" here were again rekindled those altar fires over our happy land which have spread their beacon lights throughout the world—lights which no campaign of disasters can now extinguish, and no succeeding glory can eclipse. In the inspired language of our Trenton poetess (Mrs. Ellen Clementine Howarth), we will gratefully give expres.

3

sion to our own feelings. Let Jersey's sons and daughters be no longer unmindful of their monumental duty, but erect a suitable Cenotaph on the consecrated ground here best suited for it.

> 'To place his statue where the beams of morning
>   Shall earliest kiss his brow;
> Where he who led the hope of freedom's dawning
>   May herald sunrise now!
> Then build the monument—record the story,
>   And while our waters run,
> Let the first name upon our page of glory
>   Be Washington!'

"In these engagements Washington acknowledged a Providential influence. What we are now about to record, from information accurately investigated, and published by us before, seems to confirm Washington's opinion, and may be thought interesting enough to be included in the Annals of Trenton.

"Colonel Rahl, with three regiments of Hessians and a company of British light horsemen, had two warnings sent him; one, that he would be attacked on Christmas day, as before alluded to, and the other by some tory, probably from up the river, announcing Washington's crossing at McKonkey's ferry. Both failed of their design. The first was defeated in this wise: The particulars were obtained by the writer from the Potts family and General Anderson, of glorious Fort Sumter fame, and Lars Anderson, Esq., of Cincinnati, sons of the distinguished hero of our narrative, Captain Richard Clough Anderson, of Kentucky, serving in Scott's Virginia regiment during the old war.

Colonel Rahl was a brave, jovial officer, fond of music, wine, hot whiskey punch, and card playing. Stacy Potts, a Quaker, who was his host, was no card player and no Tory, but still a non-combatant, of course ; yet good for a game of chequers, or fox and geese, with an enemy, even when concealing Mr. Lanning, the Whig spy who piloted our army down the Pennington road on the 26th of December. It is stated that Colonel Rahl, after waiting all day on the look out for the enemy, was playing a game of Fox and Geese, or Chequers, with his loyal-like host, when an alarm from the outskirts of the town was heard, and springing up, he left his head-quarters, mustered his troops, found the "out-guard" attacked, as Sir William Howe reported to Lord George Germaine, and drove the enemy off, and then the next morning, he (Rahl). attacked Washington "unsuccess-fully," instead of defending the village, as Sir William Howe said he should have done, and lost his army and his life. This account appeared in the London Magazine of February, 1777. Gordon, the historian, says: Colonel Rahl dismissed his men to their quarters after the flurry on Christmas night, "and some got drunk." This is very probable. Mr. Potts stated that the brave Colonel never returned that night to finish the game, but next morn-ing, after he was mortally wounded, he was brought to his house and died there.

"The company of Virginia regulars before alluded to, under command of Captain Anderson, were on a scout by permission of General Stevens, but without Washing-ton's knowledge, and approaching Trenton, on Christmas evening, attacked and wounded the picket, took their guns, and hastily marched back to join the army on its way to surprise the Hessians. They and their com-mander were satisfied there was no further cause of alarm and were probably off their guard, although Sir

William Howe's report states that Colonel Rahl was
advised of Washington's approach and made an unsuc-
cessful attack upon our troops. General Washington
says in his report the enemy 'never made any regular
stand." The surprise, however, was complete, more so,
perhaps, than our General apprehended. for, it is said'
he was angry with General Stevens, when Anderson's
attack was told him, fearing he had alarmed Rahl. and
that his plan would be defeated. Captain Anderson,
however, was afterwards complimented for his brave and
well-timed manœuvre. Washington, with many a noble
General, has been free to admit

> ' There's a Divinity that shapes our ends,
> Rough-hew them how we will.'

"Another anecdote connected with this 'strange eventful history' is related on good authority, and the belief
in it is quite current here. The reported statement of
Mr. Potts that Colonel Rahl never returned to his head-
quarters after he left his house on Christmas night, and
Sir William Howe's belief that he was apprised of Washington's approach, render the truth of the following
story possible, if not probable:

"It is said that in those times that tried men's souls,
the taste of American Independence did not agree with
some stomachs as well as British punch and old Jamaica.
In the old mansion still standing at the corner of Warren and State streets, lately occupied as a liquor store
by our deceased friend Mr. Norcross, and now converted
into a wholesale apothecary store by its proprietor, S. K.
Wilson, for Dr. George McDonald. there resided a
respected friend of the Tories in the Revolution, named
Abraham Hunt. On the night of Christmas. 1776. when

loyal subjects. of his most Christian Majesty, George the III, were supposed to be in the best spirits, it was natural that they should wish their British friends and allies, tempted by the gold and *coppers* that they would get for cutting Yankee throats, to partake of the spirits of the times. and to join in a game of brag, perhaps. Colonel Rahl. it is reported, after his great alarm was succeeded by the brilliant victory over the ragamuffin Yankees at his outpost, could not or would not resist having a good time at Mr. Hunt's hospitable home.

> "Cards. wine and dice, no Coffee-house nor Iun,
> But tea and scandal cheered the souls within!"

The wintry night was whiled away, and towards morning whist and whiskey-punch. monopolized the ring. Washington and state affairs were not thought of. The colored man in charge of the door was ordered to let no one go out or in. This was the custom of the times. as we have heard the venerable Charles Cotesworth Pinckney say, who was a General in these matters as well as in diplomacy, when he told Talleyrand, "Millions for defence, but not one cent for tribute." Well! not to be too garrulous, we will here say the janitor obeyed orders. After midnight, Colonel Rahl being in the midst of a very interesting game of whist, a rap summoned the servant to the door, (we do not remember hearing his name), who inquired, "who is there?" "A friend; I must speak to Colonel Rahl." "I must!" with the emphasis of Julius Cæsar, when he said. " *Veni, vidi, vici.*" "No!" said the janitor, "I have orders to let no one in."

Now, to make the story short, which it is not, the messenger, having a note he was ordered to deliver into the hands of Colonel Rahl. informing him that Washington was on his way down to surprise him, and having called in vain at his headquarters, had to submit to circumstances. He sent it in to him, and being delivered into the hands of the Colonel, he glanced at the superscription and thrust it into his pocket, intending to read it, but forgot it until, bleeding and dying, he was taken to his quarters, when handing out his pocket-book to Mrs. Potts, he discovered the note, and reading it, he said, with a sigh, "had I read this at Mr. Hunt's, I should not now be here."

Two reflections naturally present themselves in closing our allusions to the two wonderful occurrences which secured Washington's success in this portion of the perilous enterprise, planned by him, when both the other parts of it failed. The post of duty should never be neglected as it was in Colonel Rahl's case, for selfish gratification, and a good cause, however hopeless, may be saved by perseverance and energy, when entrusted to a General who, like Washington, never listened to despair, but relied steadfastly on the Providence of God.

BATTLE OF THE SECOND JANUARY, 1777, AND REPULSE OF CORNWALLIS.

In approaching the narrative of events long ignored in many of the early histories of the Revolutionary war and which were not put together in a credible form until they were published by me in 1856, in a pamphlet which is now out of print, I feel at liberty to furnish the readers of this Essay with full extracts from that work, repeating the arguments and details connected with this somewhat mysterious and still partly unrevealed subject for history.

But, in addition to this, I wish to add the new evidences I have since received, strongly corroborating my previous statements, and to prove by six agreeing attestations of contemporary witnesses that, in spite of the reticence of the two distinguished commanders on that occasion, (viz: Washington and Cornwallis—see their reports in Appendix,) yet their exact positions and movements of their forces have been so graphically made known by others, whose *positive* evidence is circumstantially and unitedly so much more reliable than *negative* omissions relative to their *whereabouts*, rendered prudential, it must be clear there was a desperate struggle at the Assunpink bridge with cannon and musketry on the American side, against masses of British troops rushing down a narrow street, besides a bootless attempt to cross the fords above and below the bloody scene of the conflict in Greene street.

Washington's position was his sole protection. He knew it, and the necessity of taking it; but as it was a desperate one, on the wrong side of the river, over which he had recently retreated for safety, he did not wish frightened and recreant turncoats, and deserting military cavillers to make capital by noising it abroad, even although the hazard of the die might result, as it did, favorable to his bold strategy. No doubt a resolution was taken in the Council of War after the battle, to say nothing about his position that night, if he could triumph at Princeton, or get to Brunswick as he hoped to do. Secrecy enjoined on his officers then is manifest and was not to be broken by them afterwards *officially*. The other lookers on, however, and participants in the fight told the truth about it.

Cornwallis was in every way out-generaled—did not accomplish anything and had to keep dark, as Napoleon did running away from Russia, until he got back to Paris. He did, however, say to the Abbe de Pratt, that "*there was but one step from the sublime to the ridiculous*," and Cornwallis might have told Sir William Howe, his sublime movement on a small scale, turned out rather ridiculous, and like Napoleon's mistake, eventuated in a failure at last, as Yorktown witnessed.

After the exploit of capturing the Hessians which so astonished Sir William and Lord Howe as to

> "Confound their politics
> And frustrate their knavish tricks,"

our infant Republic ventured once more to look out of its cradle with an air of Independence. "But Washington knew the perils that still surrounded him. He could judge how best to turn the enemy's panic to our own advantage, and to prepare for that vindictive reaction which was sure to stimulate the haughty British lords who, whilst hunting the lion, had presumed to sell his skin. Angered and excited, for he was not imperturable when great occasions required his being aroused, he wished to give back some blows like those he had received, whilst his blood was warm. He therefore lost no time in arranging a plan, in connection with Generals Cadwalader, Putnam, Dickinson, and Mifflin, to follow up the attack of the Hessians, and to drive the British, if possible, out of this State.

"That he was not incited to this extra hazardous undertaking, which all military critics have ventured, in spite of its success, to consider a departure from his own usually prudent policy. by a desire to exhibit *decision*,

the doubt of which, as a military chief, he must have
felt prompted to rebuke, I shall not assert nor deny.
But I will certainly maintain, that he always had the
good of his country most at heart, and however hazardous this second adventure to measure swords with the
enemy on the fields of Trenton was, whatever mixture
of feeling and purpose there was in his own breast, there
never was a time in the whole management of any
threatening disaster, when his genius shewed itself more
resplendent, and his military tactics more decidedly
efficacious. His early history, his whole life, had exhibited that invincible constitution of soul that rose with the
difficulties it had to encounter, and he wanted then to
inspire the country with a confidence in him and in their
cause, which should know no fear, and, as far as his
guarantee for success could go, his own life, his ample
fortune, and unblemished reputation were then cheer-
fully staked.

"On the 29th of December he wrote Congress of his
intended project 'to pursue the enemy in his retreat,
to try to break up more of their quarters, and in every
instance to adopt such measures as the exigency of our
affairs require and our situation will justify.' This is
what Wilkinson calls being 'infected with a chivalrous
spirit.'

"The eclat which attended the first achievement at
Trenton, the capture of a thousand of the ferocious Hessians, for a while eclipsed all subsequent events. This
was one cause why the second, less brilliant, but equally
hazardous and much more important engagement, on
the same ground, should be passed over slightingly, both
in the private reports of it as well as in the imperfect

4

representations of those who have alluded to it in history.

"There is another cause for the meagre reports of the killed and wounded in these several encounters, and of their being ignored in the official returns, or rather of there being no published returns of what took place in these continued skirmishes prior to the attack and capture of the British, near Princeton. Both armies were on flying marches, and their commanders, British as well as American, must have both found themselves in bad positions. Now we know how tenacious military men are of honor and cautious of exposing their mistakes. It is sometimes even as impolitic to boast of a victory as to acknowledge a defeat. Besides, the British army concealed its loss of men by being on the advance all the time it was being attacked by our retreating forces. which continued several hours, and they undoubtedly picked up their killed and wounded, whether few or many, and left us no account of them. When the attack on our troops, posted South of the Assunpink, took place, their loss was easier to be reckoned. Now, because a few old people in this neighborhood do not remember any thing about there being any fight on this occasion, whilst others do, and have published the particulars of it, some having been in the battle, some looking on, and one who was engaged in it having published its very interesting details in the same month when it took place, I do not see that we need to be in any doubt about the matter.

"With as much brevity as possible, I will now endeavor to show that there were many severe skirmishes or fights, which continued from before noon until dark, in which a good many of the pursuers must have been killed, and that Lord Cornwallis was not only baffled, but eventually met with a severe repulse in trying to pass the Assunpink on the 2nd. besides being completely outgeneraled on the morning of the 3d of January. My evidence is derived from reliable and authentic reports from those who were participants in. or observers of what was going on at the time, and I shall certainly endeavor to state them fairly, leaving others to form their own opinions.

"Three days after the first victory at Trenton. Washington set out with the troops under his command to cross the Delaware in boats. but it was two days before they all could be got over. The weather was soft and the ice drifting. and the roads almost impassable with mire and snow. On their arrival they took up the quarters which the Hessians had occupid the week before. Here they were joined by about three thousand of the new levies under Generals Cadwalader and Mifflin. and a part of the Massachusetts and Rhode Island brigade, commanded by the gallant Colonel Hitchcock. who died of fatigue and suffering the week after at Morristown. This junction of the old and new troops took place on Tuesday night. the last day of the year, and also the last day of service of nearly all the old soldiers whom Washington had to depend on.

"Early on the morning of the 2nd of January. 1777. General Cornwallis, with Grant's division. left Princeton. Their outposts extended to the eight mile run. The whole army amounted to about eight thousand troops. part of which, under General Leslie. were to be posted on the road. and another part was left to follow next

morning from Princeton.   Probably about five thousand
were to move forward to break up General Washington's quarters at Trenton.   The usual prestige of the
British, with their proud red coats and glittering arms,
and St. George's banner heralding their devoted attach-
ment to loyalty and booty, had lately received such a
check from the " ragamuffin rebels," that redoubled ven-
geance now lighted up their maddened countenances, as
they cursed the cowardly Hessians, and were ready to
pounce on their presumptuous assailants.   Cornwallis
was determined to make an end of such troublesome
traitors, who would neither stay beaten, nor submit to
royal pardon, nor consent to tempting bribes. Annihila-
tion was the only remedy.

   " Washington, aware of his enemy's real superiority
in numbers, and condition of his troops, made prompt
and determined exertions to check his advance, and to
provide as strong a position as possible for his own
army.   The arrangements for the day were as follows:

   " The main body of the army was posted on the south
side of the Assunpink—the tributary, but on this occasion the rival of the proud Delaware in story.   Its
sloping bank above the bridge, eastward, was soon
thrown up into parapets, so that the infantry could fire
diagonally in line over each other's heads.   Near the
bridge below, the only one then in Trenton, over which
a part of the Hessian dragoons escaped the week before
to Bordentown, and the same where Washington was
crowned with flowers by the ladies of Trenton, in 1789—
there stood, in 1777, the old Stacy or Trent Stone Mill.
Below this, on the high ground on the opposite side of
the road, to the south-west, Knox's battery was posted,

in a capital position for firing up Greene street, to check
the enemy's advance, as well as to defend the fords on
either side of the bridge. Still lower down the stream
there was a field on its margin, extending towards the
flats of the Delaware. On this ground Washington
directed Colonel Hitchcock's New England regiment to
take their stand and guard the fords where they could
easily have been crossed, and would probably have been,
but for their determined show of resistance. A small
space of the artillery ground on that occasion is still
unoccupied near the street, on the top of the hill next
the bridge. All the residue, with the field below, is now
covered with thriving factories, foundries, flour mills, &c.

* " Washington having thus taken his position, dis-
patched a strong division under General Fermoy, with a
battery of six guns, under charge of the brave Captain
Forest, Colonel Hand's riflemen, Colonel Scott's Virginia
regiment, and the German battalion of Houssiger, to
five-mile run, on the Princeton road, where they were
posted on the night preceding the battle, with pickets
extending to what is now Lawrenceville. It was evidently Washington's intention to check the advance of
Cornwallis, to thin his ranks and by harrassing him
during his march, to weaken his confidence, and to
decoy him adroitly in pursuit of a retreating but galling
adversary, with as much procrastination as practicable,
so that the day might ·be consumed before he could
reach our fortified position on the Assunpink, toward
which Washington wished his attention exclusively
invited in order not to have his rear so exposed as to
place our army in a *cul de sac*. To prevent this, he

* Wilkinson, vol. 1.

ordered General St. Clair with part of his brigade to
guard the fording places of that river *above the town* with
two guns, which actually prevented the enemy's flank-
ing parties from crossing there. If these stray hawks,
who got upon that sight, had not been called off to pursue the game ahead. it might have been a sorry day
with our army, as good a quarry as our General was.
He must infallibly have been caught. if by his sagacity
he had not used the most admirable skill and precaution
in the whole arrangement of this almost ignored part of
the day's achievements, eclipsed, as they scarcely were,
by those of the succeeding night.

"As these precautionary orders were given early,
with the full foresight of what might be the ultimate
fortunes of the day. could not Washington have had
then revolving in his mind that famous night retreat to
Princeton, which was afterwards adopted in a council of
war. and which. General Wilkinson says. was first proposed by General St. Clair?

"I do not presume to say that this was not so, for
that brave old comrade of Washington in former wars.
however unfortunate afterwards, was ever trusted and
beloved by him, and on this occasion was particularly
confided in as he was well acquainted with the ground
in this neighborhood. However, in the throes of that
agonizing night. whoever may have suggested the
Cœsarean operation of delivering the army out of its
perilous situation, and eventually causing a separation
fatal to the hopes of the mother country, let it be
remembered that *many* may be entitled to a share of
distinction, whose particular merits may never have been
justly recorded in history: but it would be invidious to

deny any who assisted in it, especially the barefooted soldiers, whatever share of glory they were richly entitled to.

" The first shot that was exchanged between the two outposts of the British and Americans on the morning of the 2nd, killed a Hessian Yager, pursuing a Mr. Hunt towards Lawrenceville, within the American picket. Apprized by this of the enemy's approach, our troops at five-mile run were called to arms and retired slowly until orders were received from Washington to dispute every inch of ground without too great risk of the guns. Colonel Hand with his riflemen, and Major Miller with the guards, and Forest with his six pieces of artillery, at once faced about and made a stand that checked the enemy's advance, and this they continued to do, with much loss to the British as they advanced, until they reached Shabbakong, a little rivulet about two miles from Trenton, where there was a thick wood extending on one side of the road nearly a mile in depth.   Here Hand posted his riflemen, and with Major Miller's guards on the left, waited under cover of the trees until the British came within point-blank shot, and then opening a heavy fire, drove them back with great loss and confusion.

" As they retreated, their flank and advanced guards were pursued by our riflemen.

" The boldness of this manœuvre completely checked the whole British forces, and by threatening them with a general attack, caused Cornwallis to form them in order of battle, and bringing up his artillery he scoured the wood for a half an hour to dislodge our riflemen. Before this whole arrangement could be got through with, full two hours were lost to him and gave our fatigued soldiers time to refresh themselves and prepare for another such skirmish, or more properly repulse. The British finally got by the wood and leaving the Shabbakong in their rear, wheeled to the high ground on the right.

"On the North side of Trenton, about a mile from where the town then was, there is a ravine leading to the Assunpink. On the South-west side of the hollow the advance of the Americans was posted in strong force, having Forest's battery with about six hundred men to defend their position. Here they made their last stand. Here Washington with Greene and Knox, were on the ground about three o'clock, and after thanking the troops, especially the artillery and riflemen, for their bravery, and encouraging them to make as bold a resistance as they could on that ground, the General returned to marshal his troops for the defence on the Assunpink. He was then expecting, undoubtedly, that *there* would be *the* battle on which depended the fortunes of his country, and his own reputation, with the probable sacrifice of his life, and the total destruction or capture of his devoted officers and soldiers! He was mounted on his proud white charger, as undaunted as himself, and, if Trumbull's picture of the scene is correct, they both seemed to breath defiance and to anticipate victory; for, after dismounting and taking his stand on the West side of the bridge, which old Mr. Howland states, was precisely his position, as the sun was about setting, the artist paints him with his head uncovered, and standing as if waiting the crisis

'Like Teneriffe or Atlas unremoved.'*

* See Trumbull's Picture and Memoirs.

"The last skirmish with the British in the outskirts of the town was now waxing warm. Wilkinson states that they brought up a battery to attack ours, and when the action had continued twenty or twenty-five minutes, they partially displayed column, and advanced in line. The firing of musketry was soon mingled with that of artillery, but the enemy's forces being three times more numerous than ours, he continued his advance until he forced us to retire by the bridge across the Assunpink. (He then says a cannonade ensued, &c. But his account is somewhat ambiguous and conflicting).

"The main conflict of the day has now to be described. I shall avail myself of four several accounts of it, and the reader will be able to judge whether their concurrent testimony makes it out worthy the name of a battle. At all events it was a repulse, and not a bloodless one to our enemies, nor of small advantage to the Americans, who kept the field as long as they thought proper to hold it. This is certainly written in the king's chronicles, and *that field, is it not still with us ?*

"General Wilkinson, who was an eye witness of this 'day's disaster' to Cornwallis, which was so visible on the morrow 'in his morning face' states that he had a fair flank view of this little combat near the bridge, from the opposite side of the Assunpink, and recollected perfectly that the sun had set and evening was so far advanced that he could distinguish *the flames from the muzzles of our muskets.*

*"A writer in the Connecticut Journal, who was an officer in the battle, states on the 22d of the same month in which it was fought, that 'on Thursday the enemy

* Copied from Howe and Barber's New Jersey.

5

marched down in a body of four or five thousand men
to attack our people at Trenton. Not long before sun-
set they marched into the town and after reconnoitering
our situation, drew up in a solid column in order to force
the bridge, which they attempted to do with great vigor,
at *three* several times, and were as often broken by our
artillery and obliged to retreat, and to give over the
attempt *after suffering great loss, supposed to be at least one
hundred and fifty killed.'*"

An eye witness published an account in the Princeton
Whig, November 4th, 1842, from which the following
was selected by Howe and Barber:

"Washington's army was drawn up on the east side
of the Assunpink, with its left on the Delaware river,
and its right extending a considerable way up the mill
pond along the face of the hill, where the factories now
stand. The troops were placed one above the other, so
that they appeared to cover the whole slope from bot-
tom to top, which brought a great many muskets within
shot of the bridge. Within seventy or eighty yards of
the bridge and directly in front of, and in the road, as
many pieces of artillery as could be managed were stationed. * * * The British did not delay the attack.
They were formed in two columns, the one marching
down Greene street to carry the bridge, and the other
down Main (now Warren) street, to ford the creek, near
where the lower bridge now stands. From the nature
of the ground, and being on the left, this attack (simul-
taneously with the one on the bridge) I was not able to
see. It was repelled, and eye witnesses say the creek
was nearly filled with their dead. The other column
moved slowly down the street, with their choicest troops

in front. When within about sixty yards of the bridge they raised a shout and rushed to the charge. It was then that our men poured upon them with musketry and artillery, a shower of bullets, under which however, they continued to advance, though their speed was diminished, and as the column reached the bridge, it moved slower and slower until the head of it was gradually pressed nearly over, when our fire became so destructive that they broke their ranks and fled. It was then that our army raised a shout, and such a shout I have never since heard; by what signal or word of command, I know not. The line was more than a mile in length and from the nature of the ground the extremes were not in sight of each other, yet they shouted as one man. The British column halted instantly; the officers restored the ranks, and again they rushed to the bridge, and again was the shower of bullets poured upon them with redoubled fury. This time the column broke before it reached the centre of the bridge, and their retreat was again followed by the same hearty shout from our line. They returned a third time to the charge, but it was in vain. We shouted after them again, but they had enough of it. It is strange that no account of the loss of the English was ever published, but from what I saw it must have been great."

In addition to the three preceeding statements, which agree as to there having been an attack by Cornwallis on the American forces at the bridge, and a repulse by means of cannon and fire-arms. I now introduce the testimony of the fourth witness, who was the late venerable John Howland, President of the Historical Society of Rhode Island, a veteran of Revolutionary distinction,

who was in the fight on the Assunpink in 1777, and
whose particular details of many events of thrilling interest, and whose graphic description of the locality is
so remarkably accurate, I quote largely from his letter
published in 1831 :

"This was the time which tried both body and soul.
We had, by order of the General, left our tents at Bristol,
on the other side of the Delaware. We were standing on
frozen ground, which was covered with snow. The hope
of the Commander-in-Chief was sustained by the character of these half-frozen, half-starved men, that he could
persuade them to volunteer for another month. He made
the attempt, and it succeeded. He directed, or requested,
General Mifflin to address or harangue our brigade; he
did it well, although he made some promises, perhaps
without the advice of General Washington, which were
never fulfilled. He said all or every thing which should
be taken from the enemy during the month, should be
the property of the men, and the value of it divided
among them. These promises, although they had no
weight or effect in inducing the men to engage, ought
to have been fulfilled, though, at the time they were
made, no one could suppose it probable we could take
stores or baggage from the enemy, who had six men to
our one then in Jersey. The request of the General
was assented to by our unanimously poising the firelock
as a signal. Within two hours after this vote we were
on our march for Trenton, which place we had left two
days previous. From the badness of the road, the dark-
ness of the night, and accidents to the artillery carriages,
or the falling of a horse, &c., we consumed the whole
night in the march, and quartered in the morning in

houses from which the Hessians had been taken the week before. When we had kindled a fire and were collecting from our knapsacks or pockets a stray remnant of bread or tainted pork, and thus taking our little share of rest or comfort, the drums beat, and we were immediately paraded. Most of those who have attempted to write a history of the war, have given some, though imperfect, accounts of the transactions of this day. Lord Cornwallis was on the march from Princeton with, as it was said, ten thousand men to beat up our quarters. Here was the whole army of the United States, which was supposed to amount to about four thousand men, commanded by His Excellency General Washington, Mifflin, Sullivan, Greene, Knox, &c.

"Our troops were posted on the south side of a brook or small river which crosses the town near the south end and enters the Delaware—a continuation of the main street crossed this little river over a stone bridge. It was evidently the purpose of General Washington to induce Cornwallis to approach and enter the town at the north end; for this purpose a company of artillery and a picket was placed on the road leading from Princeton, who were attacked by the advance of the British. Our brigade was ordered to cross the bridge and march through the main town street, to cover the retreat of the artillery and picket, into and through the north end of the town. This was towards the close of the day. We met them, and opened our ranks to let them pass through; we then closed in a compact and rather solid column, as the street through which we were to retreat to the bridge was narrow, and the British pressed closely on our rear. Part of the enemy

pressed into a street between the main street and the
Delaware, and fired into our right flank at every space
between the houses. When what was now our front
arrived near the bridge which we were to pass, and
where the lower or Water street formed a junction with
the main street, the British made a quick advance in an
oblique direction to cut us off from the bridge; in this
they did not succeed, as we had a shorter distance in a
direct line to the bridge than they had, and our artillery,
which was posted on the south side of the brook, between the bridge and the Delaware, played into the
front and flank of their columns, which induced them
to fall back The bridge was narrow, and our platoons
were, in passing it, crowded into a dense and solid
mass, in the rear of which the enemy were making
their best efforts. The noble horse of General Washington stood with his breast pressed close against the
end of the west rail of the bridge, and the firm, com-
posed, and majestic countenance of the General inspired
confidence and assurance in a moment so important and
critical. In this passage across the bridge, it was my
fortune to be next the west rail, and arriving at the end
of the bridge, I pressed against the shoulder of the
General's horse and in contact with the boot of the General. The horse stood as firm as the rider, and seemed
·to understand that he was not to quit his post and station. When I was about half-way across the bridge, the
General addressed himself to Colonel Hitchcock, the
commander of the brigade, directing him to march his
men to *that field* and form them immediately, or instantly,
or as quick as possible—which of the terms he used I
am not certain—at the same time extending his arm

and pointing to a little meadow at a little distance, on the south side of the creek or river, and between the road and the Delaware. This order was promptly obeyed, and then we advanced to the edge of the stream, facing the enemy, who soon found it prudent to fall back under cover of the houses. What passed at the bridge while we were forming as directed, I of course did not witness, but understood that as soon as our brigade had passed, the cannon which had been drawn aside to leave us a passage, were again placed at the end of the bridge and discharged into the front of the enemy's column, which was advancing towards it, at the same time several pieces placed at the right and left of the bridge, *with musketry at the intervals, took them partly in flank.* They did not succeed in their attempt to cross the bridge, and although the creek was fordable between the bridge and the Delaware, they declined attempting a passage there in the face of those who presented a more serious obstruction than the water.

"Night closed upon us, and the weather, which had been mild and pleasant through the day, became intensely cold. On one hour—yes, or forty minutes, commencing at the moment when the British troops first saw the bridge and creek before them—depended the all-important, the all-absorbing question, whether we should be Independent States or conquered rebels! Had the army of Cornwallis, within that space have crossed the bridge or forded the creek, unless a miracle intervened, there would have been an end of the American army. If any fervent mind should doubt this, it must be from his not knowing the state of our few, half-starved, half-frozen, feeble, worn-out men, with old fowl-

ing pieces for muskets, and half of them without bayonets, and the States so disheartened, discouraged, or
poor, that they sent no reinforcements, no recruits to
supply the places of this handful of men." *   *   *   *

The following remarkable confirmation of the preceding accounts published in my "WASHINGTON AND HIS
ARMY" in 1856, I obtained the year after from Rev. Dr.
Styles' Diary, in the library at New Haven. The
article was copied by me and printed in the Weekly
STATE GAZETTE of this city, August 15th, 1857. Being
originally published by a gentlemen (supposed to be Dr.
Rush or Mr. Armstrong), then in attendance upon General Mercer "near Princeton," and written within the
same week the events narrated took place, they are
entitled to great credit, as is the short letter from General Greene to Thomas Paine, copied from the same
Diary, as evidence of the great losses the enemy suffered.

LETTER FROM A GENTLEMAN OF GREAT WORTH IN THE
AMERICAN ARMY TO THE PRINTER OF THE MARYLAND
JOURNAL, DATED NEAR PRINCETON, JAN. 7TH, 1777.

"On the 2d instant, intelligence was received by
express that the enemy's army was advancing from
Princeton towards Trenton, where the main body of our
forces was then stationed. Two brigades, under Generals
Stephens and Fermoy, had been detached several hours
before from the main body to Maidenhead, and were
ordered to skirmish with the enemy during their march,
and retreat to Trenton as occasion should require. A
body of men under command of Colonel Hand were also
ordered to meet the enemy, by which means their march
was so much retarded as to give ample time for our

forces to form and prepare to give them a warm reception upon their arrival. Two field pieces, planted upon a hill at a small distance from the town, were managed with great advantage, and did considerable execution for some time; after which they were ordered to retire to the station occupied by our forces on the south side of the bridge, over the little river (the Assunpink), which divides the town into two parts, and opens at right angles into the Delaware. In their way through the town the enemy suffered much by an incessant fire of musketry from behind the houses and barns. The army had now arrived at the northern side of the bridge, whilst our army was drawn up in order of battle on the southern side. *Our cannon played very briskly* from this eminence, and were returned as briskly by the enemy. In a few minutes after the cannonade began, *a very heavy discharge of musketry ensued, and continued for ten or fifteen minutes*; during this action a party of men were detached from our right wing to secure a part of the river which it was imagined, from the motions of the enemy, they intended to ford. This detachment arrived at the pass very opportunely, and effected their purpose. *After this* the enemy made a feeble and unsupported attempt to pass the bridge, but *this likewise* proved abortive. It was now near six o'clock in the evening, and night coming on, closed the engagement.

"Our fires were built in due season, and were very numerous; and whilst the enemy were amused by these appearances, preparing for a general attack the next morning, our army marched at about one o'clock in the morning from Trenton, on the south side of the creek, to Princeton. When they arrived near the hill, about

6

one mile from Princeton, they found a body of the enemy formed upon it and ready to receive them; upon
which a spirited attack was made upon them, both with
field pieces and musketry, and after an obstinate resistance and loss of a considerable number of their men
upon the field, those of them who could not make their
escape, surrendered prisoners of war. We immediately
marched on to the centre of the town, and there took
another part of the enemy near the College. After
tarrying a very short time in town, General Washington
marched his army from thence towards Rocky Hill, and
they are now near Morristown, in high spirits, and in
expectation of a junction with the rest of our forces,
sufficiently seasonable to make a general attack upon
the enemy and prevent at least a considerable part of
them from reaching their asylum in New York.

" It is difficult to precisely ascertain the loss we have
sustained in the *two* engagements, but as near as I can
judge I think we have lost about forty men killed, and
had near double the number wounded. In the list of
the former are the brave Colonel Hazlett, Captain Ship-
pen and Captain Neal, who fell in the engagement upon
the hill near Princeton. Among the latter was Brigadier-
General Mercer, who received seven wounds in his body
and two on his head, and was much bruised by the
breach of a musket. His life was yesterday almost
despaired of, but this morning I found him much
relieved, and some of the most dangerous complaints
removed, so that I still have hopes of his recovery, and
of his being again restored to the arms of his grateful
country. He is now a prisoner upon parole.

" The loss sustained by the enemy was much greater

than ours, as was easily discovered by viewing the dead upon the field after the action. We have now one hundred of their wounded prisoners in the town, which, together with those who surrendered and were taken in small parties endeavoring to make their escape, I think must amount to the number of four hundred, chiefly British troops. Six brass cannon have fallen into our hands, a quantity of ammunition and several wagons of baggage. A Captain Leslie was found among the dead of the enemy, and was this day buried with the honors of war. A number of other officers were found on the field, but they were not known and were buried with the other dead. According to the information from the inhabitants of Princeton, the number which marched out of it to attack our army amounted to thirteen thousand men, under command of General Cornwallis. As soon as they discovered they were out-generaled by the march of General Washington, being much chagrined at their disappointment (as it seems Cornwallis intended to have cut our army to pieces, crossed the Delaware and marched without any further delay to Philadelphia), rushed with the greatest precipitation towards Princeton, where they arrived about an hour after General Washington had left, and imagining he would endeavor to take Brunswick in the same manner, proceeded briskly for that place. Our soldiers were much fatigued, the greater part of them having been deprived of their rest the two preceding nights, otherwise we might perhaps have possessed ourselves of Brunswick."

" In a letter from Major General Greene, dated in January, published in a Maryland paper, 21st January

1777, addressed to T. Paine, author of the Crisis, he says, 'The two late actions at Trenton and Princeton have put a very different face upon affairs. Within a fortnight past we have taken or killed of Howe's army between two and three thousand men. Our loss is trifling. We are daily picking up these parties. Yesterday we took seven prisoners and thirty loads of baggage.'"

My sixth testimonial of the bloody attack and repulse of Cornwallis and his army at the Assunpink bridge is contained in a letter lately received from A. Cuthbert Esq., alluded to in a previous page as the son of Captain Cuthbert, who succeeded Captain Moulder, whose battery was famous for its great service in the above fight and at Princeton. His letter is so graphic and interesting, I publish a large part of it, as he assures me its details have never been printed before and can be relied on. His own testimony as well as that of his brave and distinguished father being unquestionable :

"In 1776 the company was ordered to join in two weeks the army in Jersey. 'Moulder's boys,' consisting of eighty-two lads, from 17 to 23, were detailed at the 'crossing of the Delaware by Washington' for boatmen's duty, my father then 2d Lieutenant, having in charge the boat in which Washington himself crossed,* while Captain Moulder and the 1st Lieutenant crossed with the two guns of the Company. Moulder's age was 60, my father 25 or 26, while all the rank and file were 23 and under, all '*along-shoremen.*' Ship Carpenters, Mast, Block and Sail-makers, Riggers, &c., a hardy set of youths belonging to the water service and amply equal to any boating duty.

---

* The writer received this account of his father's taking charge of Washington's boat from Mr. Linnard, but it may not be correct.

"At the battle of the Assunpink the British in solid column charged down the main street to force the passage at the bridge, at this point the guns, long 4-pounders, of Moulder and others were stationed and did great damage to the enemy, being well placed and skillfully manned by as hardy, fearless and energetic set of youths as the army could produce. At each report a lane was opened through the British ranks and so rapid and destructive was the firing that the British troops could only be kept up to their work by the constant use of the flat of the sword by the British officers. So determined and successful was the resistance at this point that the enemy was held in check until too late in the afternoon to hope for success that day and was withdrawn to await reinforcements expected in the morning. How they were baffled and the 'tide turned' is familiar to all. At Princeton the guns of Moulder were again active, and while the British fired too high (over his men) he mowed them down in rows as if they had lain down to rest. I think the College may still bear the ball marks of his guns used to drive out some five hundred British who had there sought shelter.

"While pushing his guns up toward the College the wounded begged quarter; Moulder's men replied, 'you are safe enough, we are after live men?' handed over their canteens of whiskey and received a blessing from the wounded enemy. Moulder was here ordered to cover the retreat of our army towards Morristown by holding the enemy in check as long as safe to his men, then spike and leave his guns, and save his men by following with all speed after the main body of the army. The men refused to earn the name of 'grass-combers'

by running away from their guns and with the aid of
ropes and forty men to each ran them up the road
after the army, pursued by a Company of British horse.
Captain Samuel Morris, of First City Troop 'Quaker
Sam.' held his Company back for the protection of
Moulder's boys, and seeing their danger galloped to
their rear and formed across the road to await the
British horse, who finding their game blocked, wheeled
and returned to Princeton. Thus Moulder's guns were
saved and taken into camp at Morristown, when Moulder
was called before a Court for disobedience of orders in
risking the loss of his men. On receipt of the order to
appear before Court, the Company formed and marched
in silence to headquarters, where after a formal repri-
mand Moulder received his sword, and the boys after
three hearty cheers, struck up 'Yankee Doodle,' and
returned to their quarters in high glee. Soon after this
the waiter of the Company, lost at Princeton, drove into
camp with a cart-load of poultry, &c., duly frozen, and
very acceptable.

"While in camp here the time of the Company's enlistment expired; and as they could not be spared for
very important reasons, Washington sent to ask of them
three weeks longer service until they could be replaced
by other troops. The Company was mustered, and the
request made known and they left to consider it. Soon
after the officers in Moulder's tent heard three hearty
cheers from the men, and supposed they were glad to
go and would go home, but were soon pleasantly disap-
pointed by receiving for an answer: 'With our compliments to his Excellency, please say that "whether he
says three weeks, three months, or three years, we are

under *his* command and *at his service.*" ' After a low bow, the officers sent returned to Washington's quarters with the gratifying answer. the General receiving it with the reply—'that is all I can ask of them.'

"Subsequently 2d Lieutenant Cuthbert was promoted to 1st Lieutenant for an act of daring under the British guns at Amboy, and the 1st Lieutenant dismissed for a contrary action at the time. Captain Moulder retired at the age of 65, in 1780, when my father received the Commission as Captain of the Company as shown to you. Higher grade in the army was offered but declined—he being a man of war in *war only*—at other times a man of peace. His property and that of his mother-in-law was destroyed by the enemy while here. His expenditures for his Company and losses in various ways footed up about $44,000, but was never claimed; nor would our mother receive some $6.000 or more, due her under the law of 1838, as widow's pension.

A. CUTHBERT.

My six testimonials of this long ignored conflict here terminate. In my address of 1856, I remarked:

"From the foregoing accounts it seems to me an unquestionable fact that there was severe fighting, and that the lists of killed and wounded must have been large, although the official reports of the action, both English and American, are very curt and unsatisfactory in their allusions to it. That it was costly to the British and ended ingloriously for their commander, as well as exceedingly critical in its consequences to the Americans, and invested Washington's military fame with a note of interrogation as well as of admiration, cannot be doubted. Napoleon once remarked of General Blucher, that he never vanquished him over night that he did not always return to the fight the next morning. Washington in this instance was not vanquished, although some say he ought to have been; but he was certainly a victor, and by his admirable strategical arrangements to escape out of his perplexing difficulty, both before and after Cornwallis gave up the contest at the bridge, he deserves imperishable renown. The guarding of the fords above the town, as already alluded to, and the costly repulses the British met with as they advanced and were lured towards that fatal bridge-fight, just late enough to cause Cornwallis to forego present advantage and to create a blind confidence in an easy triumph on the morrow, deserve particular consideration, and whether few or many fell in accomplishing the repulses of that day's work, must now be a matter of little moment. Blank cartridges certainly would not have done it; and if cannon and musket balls could speak, enough of them have been picked up to tell the story of a fight at the bridge, beside what had been done on the Shabbakong and along the road. I have not a doubt that our enemies, although they concealed their losses during this day's various engagements, suffered more in killed and wounded than they did in both the battles of Trenton and Princeton. We may reasonably estimate their loss at 500 at least, besides incidentally producing, in connection with other losses to their cause about this time, which were wholly incalculable, the release of thousands of the oppressed citizens of this State, who were soon afterwards converted into its unfaultering defenders.

"When Cornwallis found himself so roughly handled

and repulsed on attempting to cross the Assunpink, a fatal delusion seemed to possess his mind. He told his officers 'he had the enemy safe enough and could dispose of them next morning.' For these reasons he proposed that the troops should make fires, refresh themselves, and take repose. General Grant and other officers, and the troops, without doubt, coincided in this conclusion, and thus the British army indulged in that repose which 'knew no waking' until the thunder of the cannon at Princeton aroused them from their morning's slumber, and the frightened Cornwallis, having played the Lord with the then loyal ladies of Trenton, and exchanged salutations with the tories at the splendid new mansion on the south-west corner of Greene and State streets, (where now stands the iron-pillared store of independent Americans, who dare to sell hob-nails contrary to the act of Parliament at that time,) found himself summoned by the morning drum-beat to give up his dream of conquest, and to admit for once that Washington, whom Sir William Erskine styled the night before, 'an old fox,' had disdained to be caught, even by a lordly sportsman.

"Whilst sleep and refreshing repose were thus wearing away the hours of a winter's night with our enemies at Trenton, a very different state of things—a most ominous and anxious apprehension of to-morrow's events—filled the minds of every weary officer and soldier on the other side of the Assunpink. There watched they with patience, still ready to do and dare everything for their country which their beloved commander should require of them. The star-studded canopy of heaven was the only tent they had that night; the miry ground

7

mixed with snow, was the only place afforded them for repose, until a rude cold wind stiffened it into seats which they could use until their orders for the night should be received. But the protecting hand of Providence was still stretched out over them, and it is not unreasonable to suppose that some minds among them may have looked up to the firmament over their heads and thanked God for giving this country no cheap independence, and for making them willing to become martyrs to achieve it.

"'The camp fires were soon lighted, and all was conjecture what was to be done on the morrow. As hour after hour passed away, there was naturally some impatience, but no insubordination. A council of war was called at St. Clair's head-quarters, in a small house still standing on the south side of the road, (occupied in 1856 by Miss Douglass,) near the German Church. Washington's quarters were rendered untenable by the enemy's attack. He was surrounded by difficulties, and never did he so much before require and receive the advice and confidence of his officers. The danger seemed to hang over and threaten to crush them all. He, however, maintained his own firm hold of calm confidence in God and the justice of his cause, and like that lofty tower, the seeming wonder of Pisa, which ever appears about to fall, still ever firmly stands, he inspired all hearts with confidence.

"Of several plans proposed at that meeting, the boldest one was unanimously adopted, to wit: by a retrograde movement to attack the over-confident enemy in his rear, to beat up his quarters at Princeton, and, if possible, capture his stores at New Brunswick. Orders were immediately given to put the troops under march, with the least noise and delay possible, and to send off what guns, baggage, and stores were not wanted, to Bordentown.*

"The enemy's watch-fires were kindled only about one hundred and fifty yards from the American camp. Washington directed his sentinels to take the fences and keep up brisk fires opposite to them until morning, and then to retreat to Princeton.† Men were also engaged to throw up intrenchments as near the British pickets as possible, and to make evident preparations for the morrow. All was now going on stilly and actively as possible, and fortunately, before midnight there was, what Washington called, a providential change in the weather. The roads became hard enough to support the artillery, and for the troops to march on frozen ground. Washington and his officers went the rounds among them and encouraged them to be firm and quiet.

"Then was presented a scene on the banks of our peaceful little Assunpink which is well realized by Shakespeare's description of Henry V., whose army, by the way, was about the same size, and in as miserable a condition at Agincourt, before his victory, as Washington's was here.

> ' From camp to camp, through the foul womb of night,
> The hum of either army stilly sounds,
> That the fixed sentinels almost receive
> The secret whispers of each other's watch.
> Fire answers fire—
>
> O ! now who will behold
> The noble captain of this ruin'd band,
> Walking from watch to watch, from tent to tent,
> Let him cry, praise and glory on his head !'

* See Reed's letter to Putnam, in "Spark's Life of Colonel J. Reed "

† Dr. Ramsay calls this a "pillar of fire to hide our army from the pursuit of the enemy."

"I need not give a detailed account of what our brave countrymen suffered and achieved on their march to and after they arrived at Princeton. These events have been faithfully and graphically related by others," but the reader will excuse what follows.

THE NIGHT MARCH AND FLANK MOVEMENT FROM TRENTON TO PRINCETON.

This was an eventful and trying period, causing perhaps as much persevering energy and patriotic fidelity as any during this memorable campaign, and like the capture of the Hessians, it ushered in a dawn even more glorious, ending in a triumph ensuring more securely the success of our life-struggle for our almost abandoned Independence. In its consequences, certainly, connected with the victory at Princeton, completing three acts of the exciting drama, which was then being performed, few historic events can surpass it, however many more heroic achievements in "war's vast art," celebrated in ancient and modern times, may eclipse it.

Mr. Howland gives his vivid description of and participation in this night adventure as follows:

"The march that night from Trenton to Princeton is well known. It was not by the direct road; a considerable part of it was by a new passage, which appeared to have been cut through the woods, as the stubs were left from two to five inches high. We moved slow on account of the artillery, frequently coming to a halt, or stand still, and when ordered forward again, one, two, or three men in each platoon, would stand, with their arms supported, fast asleep; a platoon next in the rear advancing on them, they, in walking, or attempting to move, would strike a stub and fall. Our proceedings at

Princeton are matters of history, except one circumstance, which has a bearing on the present question—that is, the Commander-in-chief took the commander of our brigade by the hand, after the action—expressing his high approbation of his conduct and that of the troops under his command, and wished him to communicate his thanks to his officers and men.

"Besides the prisoners taken at Princeton, there were a number of wagons loaded with the army baggage. I suppose it was about noon when we left Princeton with the prize goods and prisoners; we marched quick, as the advance guard of the British army whom we had left the night before at Trenton, were said to be close in our rear, following us as they supposed to Brunswick, the headquarters of General Howe, but in three or four miles we turned a square corner and proceeded north, towards Somerset Court-House. The British continued on to Brunswick. Ten or eleven o'clock at night we arrived at the Court House, in which the prisoners were shut up. It will be remembered this was the third night's march, and under arms or marching all day. There were barely houses sufficient for the quarters of the Generals and their attendants. The troops took up their abode for the rest of the night on the frozen ground. All the fences and every thing that would burn, was piled in different heaps and burnt, and he was the most fortunate who could get nigh enough to smell the fire or smoke. The next day we continued our march towards Morristown."

I must not here repeat the oft-told narrative of the gallant deeds and costly sacrifices performed by Washington and his weary soldiers during the short, sharp contest with the desperate Mawhood and his three regiments of brave and well-armed British troops.

Washington never was more heroic—never in greater peril—never more providentially rescued from a chivalric self-devotion to patriotic honor and principle; and his pass-word, "Victory or death," was signalized by his own example,* still, all that was expected to be gained, and all which was secured by courage and strategy, was at one time in imminent danger of being lost; but, with the aid of Moulder's battery and Hitchcock's New England veterans, who rushed to the aid of the halting and flying new recruits, the doubtful and bloody triumph was soon secured, and the enemy fled in all quarters. The pursuit after them was spirited and glorious—even Washington could not resist it, but compared it to a fox chase. Thus passed the hours from dawn to mid-day, at Princeton, ninety years ago, with many interesting achievements which culminated in the eventual establishment of our country's independence, sovereignty, and universal freedom for all her citizens.

Citizens of Princeton, ye whose county bears the name of the great martyr who fell here with scores of his brave officers and men, in defence of your fatherland and your own happy homesteads, can you or your descendants ever fail to realize and appreciate the cause—the motive principle—which animated the desperate struggle that was once exhibited, like a moving panorama, upon your now peaceful fields? Tyranny no longer threatens you with submission—the rambling Stony Brook now runs cheerily on its course, as it once

* See Poem in the Appendix,

did when its little bridge bore Cornwallis' proud army
on its presumptuous march to Trenton, and brought it,
crest-fallen, back again, glad to escape from the Yankee
rebels who would not believe in British valor or loyalty.
All this has passed away, but the little stream still re-
mains, and its waves are moving on. The principles for
which our fathers fought too still remain, but the American age is moving on, and its persistent force, guided by
the Omnipotent right Reason, will give it perpetuity. To
a scholarly community I may be permitted to give a clas-
sic quotation :

——— " *Immota labescunt,*
Et quae perpetua sunt agitata manent."

No enemy now beleaguers Nassau Hall from without ;
no Church and State creed, nor monopoly of the only
true religious doctrine, can ever again hamper free and
conscientious belief in this country although they might
have done so

" In colleges and halls in ancient days,"

but progress, an earnest intelligent progress, must germ-
inate from the precious seed sown by our fathers ; and
the fields once nourished by their blood ought to give
the greatest harvest and devotion to their principles.

In closing my investigation and, as I trust, elucida-
tion of these early historical events which really possess
a National and not a mere local interest, I still feel privileged, as an adopted son of this State, to give to New
Jersey the honor of their birth-place. If, like Old
Mortality, " I have chiseled out of illegible obscurity,"
some facts that ought to be made known, and brightened
some names dimly kept out of sight at the time, hence-

forth let it be your glorious duty my countrymen, to follow Cicero's example at the tomb of Archimedes, and keep them from being moss-covered or neglected.— Monuments which, with tasteful and truthful eloquence, would perpetuate a history that might be read and admired of all men, seem not to chime in harmony with our Republican aversion to sectional and personal glorification.   Local jealousy and meaner envy block all avenues to the temple of Fame, leading to such distinction, as have been tried here and elsewhere.   The writer has worked hard, and to the best of his humble ability, to have a monument erected.   But '*nil desperandum*.' If the fight can be carried out on this line by an 'abler and better soldier," let. the triumph be secured.   On what better field can a National Cenotaph be erected than at that stand-point where was the glorious resurrection of our young Republic and where our heroic fathers

   " Plucked up its drowned honor by the locks?"

Upon such a Monument might appropriately be inscribed,

   "*Gloria majorum, posteris lumen.*"

APPENDIX.

APPENDIX.

WASHINGTON AT PRINCETON.

BY MISS C. F. ORNE.

The Assunpink was choked with dead between us and the foe;
We had mowed their ranks before our guns, as ripe grain is laid low;
But we were few, and worn and spent—many and strong were they,
And they waited but the morning dawn to fall upon their prey.
We left our camp-fires burning, that their ruddy gleaming light
Might hide from Lord Cornwallis our hurried march by night.
While fiery Erskine fretted at his leader's fond delay,
All silently and swiftly we were marching on our way.
For the British troops at Princeton our little force was bound;
We tracked with bare and bleeding feet the rough and frozen ground;
All night we hastened onward, and we spoke no word of plaint,
Though we were chilled with bitter cold, with toil and fasting faint;
We hailed with joy the sunlight, as o'er the hills it streamed,
And through the sharp and frosty air on the near homesteads beamed.
We were weary, we were hungry; before us lay good cheer,
And right gladly to the hearth-fires our eager steps drew near.
But sudden, on our startled sight, long lines of bayonets flash;
The road's a-glow with scarlet coats! The British on us dash!
The smoke-wreaths from our volleys meet; then hand to hand the fight;
Proud gallant Mercer falls; our lines are wavering in flight!
"Press on!" cries Mawhood, "by St. George! the rebel cowards fly,
We'll sweep their ranks before our charge, as storm-winds sweep the sky."

They burst with bold and sudden springs as a lion on the prey,
Our ranks of worn and weary men to that fierce rush gave way.
Black was that bitter moment, and well nigh all was lost,
But forth there sprang a god-like form between us and the host.
The martyr-fires of freedom in his flaming glances burned,
As his awful countenance sublime upon the foe he turned;
And reining up his gallant steed, alone amid the fight,
Like an angel of the Lord he stood to our astonished sight!

And instantly our wavering bands wheeled into line again,
And suddenly from either side the death-shots fell like rain.
All hearts stood still; and horror-struck was each averted eye,
For who could brook that moment's look? or who could see *him* die?
But when the smoke-clouds lifted, and still we saw him there,
Oh, what a mighty shout of joy filled all the startled air!
And tears fell like the summer showers from our bravest and our best,
As dashing up with fiery pace around him close they prest.
A moment's hand-grasp to his Aid, that told the tale of hours,
"Away! bring up the troops," he cried, "the day is wholly ours."

"Now praised be God!" from grateful lips the fervent prayers uprose,
And then, as with an eagle's swoop, we burst upon our foes.
And "Long live Washington," we cried, in answer to his shout,
As still he spurred his charger on amid the flying rout.
They broke their ranks before our charge; amain they wildly fled;
Stiff on the slopes, at Princeton, they left their hapless dead.
No more a band of weary men we followed in his track;
And bore with stern resistless force the British Lion back;
Our toilsome march, our sleepless nights, cold, hunger—what were they?
We broke the yoke of foreign power on that eventful day.
The great heart of our leader went on before us then,
And led us forth to wield the strength of more than mortal men,   .
The pulses of that noble heart a nation's life concealed,
But fate refused the sacrifice whose offer won the field.

From Graham's Magazine, for February, 1856.

[Extract from the "Gentleman's Magazine," London, Feb. 1777, folio 90.]

LETTER FROM GEN. SIR WILLIAM HOWE TO LORD GEORGE
GERMAIN, DATED NEW YORK, JANUARY, 5TH, 1777.

In consequence of the advantage gained by the enemy
at Trenton on the 26th of last month and the necessity
of an alteration in the cantonment, Lord Cornwallis
deferring his going to England by this opportunity,
went from thence to New Jersey on the 1st inst., and
reached Princeton that night, to which place General
Grant had advanced with a body of troops from Bruns-

wick and Hillsborough. Upon gaining intelligence that the enemy on receiving *reinforcements from Virginia and Maryland* and from the militia of Pennsylvania, had repast into Jersey. On the 2d Lord Cornwallis having received accounts of the rebel army being posted at Trenton advanced thither, leaving the 4th brigade under the command of Lieutenant-Colonel Mawhood at Princeton, and the 2d brigade with Brigadier-General Leslie at Maidenhead. On the approach of the British troops the enemy's forward post was drawn back upon their army which was formed in a strong position behind a creek running through Trenton. During the night of the 2d the enemy quitted its situation and marching by *Allentown* and from thence to Princeton, fell in on the morning of the 3d with the 17th and 55th Regiments on their march to join Brigadier-General Leslie at Maidenhead. Lieutenant-Colonel Mawhood, not being apprehensive of the enemy's strength, attacked and beat back the troops that first presented themselves to him. But finding them at length very superior to him in numbers, he pushed forward with the 17th regiment and joined Brigadier-General Leslie. The 55th regiment retired by the way of Hillsborough to Brunswick, and the enemy proceeding immediately to Princeton, the 40th Regulars retired to Brunswick. The loss on this occasion to his Majesty's troops is *seventeen killed and nearly two hundred wounded and missing.* Captain Leslie of the 17th was among the few killed. For further particulars I beg leave to refer your Lordship to the enclosed return. Captain Phillips of the 35th Grenadiers, returning from here to join his Company was on this day beset, between Brunswick and Princeton, by some lurking villains, who murdered him in a most barbarous manner, which is a mode of war the enemy seem, from several late instances to have adopted with a degree of barbarity that savages could not exceed.

It has not yet come to my knowledge how much the enemy has suffered, but it is certain there were many killed and wounded. and among the former a General Mercer from Virginia. The bravery and conduct of Lieutenant-Colonel Mawhood and the behavior of the regiments under his command, particularly the 17th, are highly commended by Lord Cornwallis. His Lordship finding the enemy had made this movement, and having heard the fire made by Colonel Mawhood's attack, returned immediately from Trenton; but the enemy being some hours march in front, and keeping the advantage by an immediate departure from Princeton, retreated by Kingston, breaking down the bridge behind them, and crossed the Millstone river at a bridge under Rocky Hill, to throw themselves into a strong country. Lord Cornwallis seeing it would not answer any purpose to continue his pursuit, returned with his whole force to Brunswick, and the troops on his right being assembled at Elizabethtown, Major-General Vaughn held that command. It appears by the Muster-Master-General, Sir George Osborn's return of the Hessian troops at the affair of the 26th December at Trenton, that the prisoners and missing *amounted to about seven hundred.*

N. B. Positive errors in the above statement are noted in italics. C. C. H.

TO THE PRESIDENT OF CONGRESS.

PLUCKEMIN, 5 January, 1777.

SIR :

I have the honor to inform you that, since the date of my last from Trenton, I have removed with the army under my command to this place. The difficulty of crossing the Delaware, on account of the ice, made our passage over it tedious, and gave the enemy an opportunity of drawing in their several cantonments, and assembling their whole force at Princeton. Their large pickets advanced towards Trenton, their great preparations, and some intelligence I had received, added to their knowledge that the 1st of January brought on a dissolution of the best part of our army, gave me the strongest reasons to conclude that an attack upon us was meditating.

Our situation was most critical, and our force small. To remove immediately was again destroying every dawn of hope, which had begun to revive in the breasts of the Jersey militia; and to bring those troops who had first crossed the Delaware, and were lying at Crosswicks, under General Cadwalader, and those under General Mifflin, at Bordentown, (amounting in the whole to about three thousand six hundred,) to Trenton, was to bring them to an exposed place. One or the other, however, was unavoidable. The latter was preferred, and they were ordered to join us at Trenton—which they did, by a night march, on the 1st instant. On the 2d, according to my expectation, the enemy began to advance upon us; and, after some skirmishing, the head of their column reached Trenton about four o'clock whilst their rear was as far back as Maidenhead. They attempted to pass Assunpink Creek, which runs through Trenton at different places, but finding the fords guarded, they halted and kindled their fires. We were drawn up on the other side of the creek. In this situation we remained till dark—cannonading the enemy, and receiving the fire of their field-pieces, which did us but little damage.

Having by this time discovered that the enemy were greatly superior in number, and that their design was to surround us, I ordered all our baggage to be removed silently to Burlington soon after dark; and at twelve o'clock, after renewing our fires, and leaving guards at the bridge in Trenton and other passes on the same stream above, marched by a roundabout road to Princeton, where I knew they could not have much force left, and might have stores. One thing I was certain of, that it would avoid the appearance of a retreat, (which was of consequence, or to run the hazard of the whole army being cut off,) whilst we might, by a fortunate stroke, withdraw General Howe from Trenton, and give some reputation to our arms. Happily we succeeded. We found Princeton about sun-rise, with only three regiments and three troops of light-horse in it, two of which were on their march to Trenton. These three regiments, especially the two first, made a gallant resistance, and in killed, wounded, and prisoners, must have lost five hundred men—upwards of one hundred of them were left dead on the field—and, with what I have with me, and what were taken in the pursuit and carried across the Delaware, there are near three hundred prisoners, fourteen of whom are officers, all British.

This piece of good fortune is counterbalanced by the loss of the brave and worthy General Mercer, Colonels Hazlet and Potter, Captain Neal of the artillery, Captain Fleming, who commanded the first Virginian regiment, and four or five other valuable officers, who, with about twenty-five or thirty privates, were slain in the field. Our whole loss cannot be ascertained, as many, who were in pursuit of the enemy, (who were chased three or four miles,) are not yet come in. The rear of the enemy's army lying at Maidenhead, not more than five or six miles from Princeton, was up with us before our pursuit was over; but, as I had the precaution to destroy the bridge over Stony Brook, about half a mile from the field of action, they were so long retarded there as to give us time to move off in good order for this place. We took two brass field-pieces, but, for want of horses, could not bring them away. We also took some blankets, shoes, and a few other trifling articles, burned the hay, and destroyed such other things as the shortness of the time would admit.

My original plan, when I set out from Trenton, was, to push on to Brunswick; but the harassed state of our troops—many of them having had no rest for two nights and a day, and the danger of losing the advantage we had gained by aiming at too much—induced me, by the advice of my officers, to relinquish the attempt. But, in my judgment, six or eight hundred fresh troops, upon a forced march, would have destroyed all their stores and magazines, taken (as we have since learned) their military chest, containing seventy thousand pounds, and put an end to the war. The enemy, from the best intelligence I have been able to get, were so much

9

alarmed at the apprehension of this, that they marched immediately to Brunswick without halting, except at the bridges, (for I also took up those on Mill-tone, on the different routes to Brunswick,) and got there before day.

From the best information I have received, General Howe has left no men either at Trenton or Princeton. The truth of this I am endeavoring to ascertain that I may regulate my movements accordingly. The militia are taking spirits, and, I am told, are coming in fast from this State; but I fear those from Philadelphia will scarcely submit to the hardships of a winter's campaign much longer, especially as they very unluckily sent their blankets with their baggage to Burlington. I must do them the justice, however, to add that they have undergone more fatigue and hardship than I expected militia, especially citizens, would have done at this inclement season. I am just moving to Morristown, where I shall endeavor to put them under the best cover I can. Hitherto we have been without any, and many of our poor soldiers quite barefoot, and ill clad in other respects.

I have the honor to be, &c.

Among the letters of Washington published by Sparks, from which the preceding is selected, (Vol. IV, page 258,) I find one of same date to General Putnam, in which he speaks of his difficulties and his fight at Princeton, but says little about the affair at Trenton—only that he "drew the army up on the south side of Mill Creek, and continued in that position until dusk, and then marched to Princeton." But, keeping back part of his own dilemma, he tells Putnam "to give out your strength to be twice as great as it is," showing that in time of war military men feel privileged to take great liberties in reporting or concealing their situations.

In addition to the above, I think it well to insert here the letter of Congress investing Washington with almost dictatorial powers, and likewise his letter to Messrs. Morris, Clymer. and Walton, showing his modest sense of his own importance and fidelity to the government and cause he had espoused. All was safe in his hands,

---

WASHINGTON'S DICTATORIAL POWERS.

Notwithstanding the extreme jealousy which had hitherto prevailed with most of the members of Congress, in regard to the danger of a military ascendancy, they were constrained in the present alarming aspect of affairs to invest General Washington with very extensive powers. In relation to the army, these powers constituted him in all respects a *Dictator*, according to the Roman sense of that term, as will appear by the proceedings of Congress.

"*December* 27*th*, 1776.—This Congress, having maturely considered the present crisis, and having perfect reliance on the wisdom, vigor and uprightness of General Washington, do hereby

"*Resolve*, That General Washington shall be, and he is hereby vested with full, ample, and complete powers to raise and collect together, in the most speedy and effectual manner, from any or all of these United States, sixteen battalions of infantry, in addition to those already voted by Congress; to appoint officers for the said bat-

talions of infantry; to raise, officer, and equip three
thousand light-horse, three regiments of artillery, and a
corps of engineers, and to establish their pay; to apply
to any of the States for such aid of the militia as he
shall judge necessary; to form such magazines of pro-
visions, and in such places, as he shall think proper; to
displace and appoint all officers under the rank of brigadier-general, and to fill up all vacancies in every other
department in the American army; to take, wherever
he may be, whatever he may want for the use of the
army, if the inhabitants will not sell it, allowing a rea-
sonable price for the same; to arrest and confine per-
sons who refuse to take the Continental currency, or are
otherwise disaffected to the American cause, and return
to the States of which they are citizens their names and
the nature of their offences, together with the witnesses
to prove them.

"That the foregoing powers be vested in General
Washington for and during the term of six months from
the date hereof, unless sooner determined by Congress."

The following letter was sent by Congress, as a circu-
lar, to the Governor of each of the States, accompanied
by the above resolve:

"BALTIMORE, 30th December, 1776.

"SIR :

"Ever attentive to the security of civil liberty, Congress would not have consented to the vesting of such
powers in the military department, as those which the
enclosed resolves convey to the Continental Commander-
in-chief, if the situation of public affairs did not require
at this crisis a decision and vigor which distance and

numbers deny to assemblies far removed from each other, and from the immediate seat of war.

"The strength and progress of the enemy, joined to prospects of considerable reinforcements, have rendered it not only necessary that the American forces should be augmented beyond what Congress had heretofore designed, but that they should be brought into the field with all possible expedition. These considerations induce Congress to request, in the most earnest manner, that the fullest influence of your State may be exerted to aid such levies as the General shall direct, in consequence of the powers now given him; and that your quota of battalions, formally fixed, may be completed and ordered to head-quarters with all the dispatch that an ardent desire to secure the public happiness can dictate.

"I have the honor to be, &c.,

"JOHN HANCOCK, *President.*"

TO ROBERT MORRIS, GEORGE CLYMER, AND GEORGE WAL-
TON, A COMMITTEE OF CONGRESS.

HEAD-QUARTERS, TRENTON, 1 January, 1777.

GENTLEMEN:

The messenger delivered to me the two parcels of hard money, which I suppose will turn out agreeably to the list, not having had time to count it. The sum that is lodged at Ticonderoga shall be ordered down, provided the commander in the northern department finds no better use for it there than I can make of it here.

The accounts you give me of the good effects that are likely to flow from our success at Trenton, add not a little to the satisfaction I have felt on that occasion. You are pleased to pay me many personal compliments, as if the merit of that affair was due solely to me; but I assure you the other general officers, who assisted me in the plan and execution, have full as good a right to your encomiums as myself. We are devising such measures, as I hope, if they succeed, will add as much or more to the distress of the enemy than their defeat at Trenton; and I promise myself the greatest advantages from having engaged a number of the eastern troops to stay six weeks beyond their time of enlistment by giving a bounty of ten dollars. This, I know, is a most extravagant price when compared with the time of service, but the example was set by the State of Pennsylvania with respect to their militia, and I thought it no time to stand upon trifles, when a body of firm troops, inured to danger, was absolutely necessary to lead on the more raw and undisciplined. I shall know this day how many of Colonel Glover's regiment are willing to continue in the land service. I do not expect many will be prevailed upon to stay, and I will endeavor to procure the rest for the purpose of fitting out the frigates upon the best terms I can.

The future and proper disposition of the Hessian prisoners struck me in the same light in which you view it; for which reason I advised the Council of Safety to separate them from their officers, and canton them in the German counties. If proper pains are taken to convince them how preferable the situation of their countrymen, the inhabitants of those counties, is to theirs,

I think they may be sent back in the spring so fraught with a love of liberty and property too, that they may create a disgust to the service among the remainder of the foreign troops, and widen that breach which is already opened between them and the British.

Yours, of the 31st of last month, enclosed to me sundry resolves of Congress, by which I find they have done me the honor to entrust me with powers, in my military capacity, of the highest nature and almost unlimited in in extent. Instead of thinking myself freed from all *civil* obligations by this mark of their confidence, I shall constantly bear in mind, that as the sword was the last resort for the preservation of our liberties, so it ought to be the first thing laid aside when those liberties are firmly established. I shall instantly set about making the most necessary reforms in the army; but it will not be in my power to make so great a progress, as if I had a little leisure time upon my hands. Mr. Morris has my sincere thanks for the advice and assistance he promises to give Commissary Wharton, and I beg he would remind him, that all his exertions will be necessary to support an army in this exhausted country.

I have the honor to be, &c.

The resolves of Congress, conferring the above powers, were transmitted to Washington by the Committee, who remained in Philadelphia when the Congress adjourned to Baltimore, namely: Robert Morris, Clymer, and Walton. In their letter they said:—"We find by these resolves, that your Excellency's hands will be strengthened with very ample powers; and a new reformation of the army seems to have its origin therein.

Happy it is for this country that the General of their forces can safely be entrusted with the most unlimited power, and neither personal security, liberty, nor property, be in the least degree endangered thereby."— *MS. Letter. December 31st.*

THE OLD ORCHARD APPLE TREE,

AT THE COTTAGE HOME OF C. C. HAVEN,

TRENTON, N. J.

June, 1865.

In Trenton—fair town—a time-honored name!
Where Freedom's proud stand-point crown'd Washington's fame;
Where the Hessians were caught and our young country saved—
There an old orchard showed where our torn banner waved.

Joy spread through the land when this capture took place;
And just a week after came Cornwallis's chase,
Plann'd an "*old Fox*" to catch, where his camp-fires burned;
But his Lordship ran back, and here never returned.

Fond relics and records of ancestral trees
Claim a filial respect more than fancy to please,
And such favors when met with in life's chequered lot,
Should be gratefully treasured and never forgot.

The Yankees prize dearly their old Charter Oak,
And the Stuyvesant pears yearly notice invoke;
Surely, then, the famed Orchard tree should be renowned,
This venerable relic that graces my ground!

And as such an old friend should be honored and praised,
Around its old trunk I've a summer-house raised,
Where, as long as its branches give shelter and shade,
Be its fruits here enjoyed and its roots undecayed.

And long as delight in its story is found,
With blossoms and foliage may its branches abound,
Happy birds build their nests here and merrily sing,
And children, as happy, here merrily swing.

Let me tell thee, old tree! though I live in the past,
I mean still to stand by thee as long as I last;
My children, grand-children and great-grand-children too,
Shall all cherish and praise thee with reverence due.

Still green may thy boughs be, protected by them,
Thy fruits be enjoyed as they cluster each stem;
And when thy old trunk shall be withered by time,
May their spirits be blessed in a far happier clime.